THE
FALLOUT

ATTACK ON EARTH

THE FALLOUT

GLASKO KLEIN

darbycreek

MINNEAPOLIS

Darby Creek
A division of Lerner Publishing Group, Inc.
241 First Avenue North
Minneapolis, MN 55401 USA

For reading levels and more information, look up this title at www.lernerbooks.com.

The images in this book are used with the permission of: Versionphotography/ iStock/Getty Images; briddy_/iStock/Getty Images; ilobs/iStock/Getty Images; 4khz/ DigitalVision Vectors/Getty Images.

Main body text set in Janson Text LT Std 12/17.5.
Typeface provided by Adobe Systems.

Library of Congress Cataloging-in-Publication Data

Names: Klein, Glasko, 1990– author.
Title: The fallout / Glasko Klein.
Description: Minneapolis : Darby Creek, [2018] | Series: Attack on Earth | Summary: Nina Collier is stuck in a mall with her ex-boyfriend during an alien invasion and must figure out how to find her parents and get to safety.
Identifiers: LCCN 2017046867 (print) | LCCN 2017059773 (ebook) | ISBN 9781541525832 (eb pdf) | ISBN 9781541525771 (lb : alk. paper) | ISBN 9781541526266 (pb : alk. paper)
Subjects: | CYAC: Survival—Fiction. | Extraterrestrial beings—Fiction. | Science fiction.
Classification: LCC PZ7.1.K643 (ebook) | LCC PZ7.1.K643 Fal 2018 (print) | DDC [Fic]—dc23

LC record available at https://lccn.loc.gov/2017046867

Manufactured in the United States of America
1-44561-35492-1/23/2018

TO ETHAN AND RYAN GONZALEZ—

KEEP AN EYE ON THE SKY, BOYS.

ON THE MORNING OF FRIDAY, OCTOBER 2, rings of light were seen coming down from the sky in several locations across the planet. By mid-morning, large spacecraft were visible through the clouds, hovering over major cities. The US government, along with others, attempted to make contact, without success.

At 9:48 that morning, the alien ships released an electromagnetic pulse, or EMP, around the world, disabling all electronics—including many vehicles and machines. All forms of communication technology were useless.

Now people could only wait and see what would happen with the "Visitors" next . . .

CHAPTER 1

The Visitors' ship dominated the sky overhead, but after making quite an entrance that morning, it had remained eerily quiet ever since. Still, they were up to something. The school buses the National Guard brought to the shopping mall to evacuate people had died all at once before the guardsmen even had a chance to load them. At the same time, the phones stopped working and the radio chatter that had been reliably squawking from the guardsmen's jeeps cut out.

Now one of the high school teachers, Mr. Davidson, was arguing with a guardsman about how to get the vehicles running again. Clearly they both had some strong ideas about the matter. But given that nobody had ever dealt with interstellar weaponry before, it was hard to say who the real authority was. Nina overheard the guardsman insisting it was an EMP, like they were told to expect after a nuclear strike. But Mr. Davidson was unconvinced—he didn't see any mushroom clouds anywhere. "It's a death ray—haven't you ever seen a movie before?" he kept asking.

"If it's a death ray, why aren't we dead? And where are the lasers?" the guardsman replied, doing his best to keep his cool.

Nina stopped listening. She was already tired of all the bickering. It had started as soon as the guardsmen announced that the buses were running late and that everybody needed to stay put because they weren't about to leave the pickup zone to save anybody if things went south. Even though it was still early in the afternoon, it was already easy to forget that the day had started pretty normal.

Nina's mom had been scrambling some eggs and watching her morning shows. Her dad was running late and looking for his travel mug, which he could have sworn he'd washed the night before. Nina was eating a grapefruit at the kitchen table, getting mentally prepared for another crushingly boring day of junior year. Then the day's regularly scheduled programming was interrupted by an emergency broadcast. Spaceships had appeared in the sky worldwide—the Visitors had arrived. When the local news anchors announced that school was cancelled, Nina thought it must be some kind of joke, but when they ordered the evacuation a few minutes later, she realized that there was nothing funny about any of it.

That must have been six or seven hours ago. The Colliers, along with the rest of the town, had spent most of that time waiting around in the parking lot of the Oak Grove Mall, where the National Guard was supposed to provide further instructions and transportation to a designated safe zone.

Looking back, Nina thought they should've been pretty embarrassed about the whole situation. It really wasn't a great evacuation plan. And now that it had fallen apart, hundreds of people were stuck here with their hastily packed luggage. Nina had spotted enough rolling suitcases, giant backpacks, and overflowing pillowcases to fill a whole bus all on their own. People were milling around, sitting on top of their bags, or hanging out in their no-longer-working cars: sitting ducks. If the aliens had any actual death rays and felt like testing them on this group, it would be an easy experiment.

The Visitors were doing a good job of ruining Nina's day on their own, but she was quickly learning that an alien invasion didn't make her other problems disappear. In fact, it had a way of making them worse.

"Have you heard from Steve at all today, sweetie?" Nina's mom asked her now.

Nina cringed. She really didn't want to think about Steve, her neighbor from up the street, childhood friend, and—as of last night—ex-boyfriend. She hadn't told her parents about the breakup. After all, it was none of their business.

But at that moment, as if Nina's mom

had summoned him by speaking his name, Steve sidled over to them. "Hey, Mr. and Mrs. Collier. Some day, huh?" he offered with an uncomfortable smile.

"Steven!" Nina's mom exclaimed. "So good to see that you're all right! We were just talking about you. I'm sure you two have been worried sick about each other."

Steve turned to Nina and made eye contact, which somehow managed to make things even more awkward. "Hi, Nina," he said. "How are you doing?"

Nina ran a hand across the back of her neck, pulling at her hair. "Hey, Steve, I'm fine," she said, trying to hold in an irritated sigh. "Just waiting to get out of here."

"Do you think they'll do something else, or are they just gonna sit there?" Steve asked. "The Visitors, I mean. I can't see why they would come all this way just to hang out in the sky doing nothing, but what do I know?"

Nina's mom let out a nervous laugh and said, "Well, whatever they want, I hope they're friendly."

"If they are, they sure have an odd way of showing it," said Nina's dad.

"Can we please not talk about this?" Nina asked. She spotted one of the National Guard soldiers approach a small group of others. "I wonder if they know anything new. Steve," she said, turning to him, "you should go find out."

It had struck her as a decent way to end the situation before it could get any more uncomfortable. Unfortunately it backfired stupendously. "That's a great idea!" Steve said. "Would you, um, mind coming with me to ask them? You're better at talking to people than I am."

Steve might as well have held up a sign that said *Can we please have a private conversation?* Somehow he hadn't figured out that now was *not* the time to discuss their relationship status.

"I—should probably stay with my parents," she stammered.

"Oh, it's fine, honey, go ahead," said her dad. "And while you're at it, see if they have any idea when they'll get those buses running again. I've about had it with standing around."

"Yeah, but shouldn't we stick together? I mean, it seems like a bad idea to risk getting separated, and we really don't know what's going on," Nina said, doing her best not to sound desperate.

"Oh, I'm sure your dad's right," said Nina's mom, letting out another nervous chuckle. "I think it would do you some good to stretch your legs a bit—we've been waiting around here all day. And it's not as if you're going that far. Your dad and I will be right here."

Nina decided she could diffuse the situation better without her parents listening, so she allowed herself a light sigh and put on her best imitation of a happy face. "Okay, thanks, Mom. I might feel a little better if I go for a walk."

She grabbed Steve by the arm and led him toward the cluster of guardsmen by the truck. The sooner she got him out of her parents' earshot the sooner she could have a word with him about how not cool he was currently being. He didn't offer any resistance, and they started making headway through the crowd.

But a moment later Nina's mom called out from behind them.

"Nina!"

Nina turned and saw her mother following them, waving the small canvas bag filled with Nina's diabetes supplies. Nina always hated how her mother took such an active role in managing her condition. Nina was the one who had been living with it since she was twelve years old, and at almost seventeen she knew a thing or two about taking care of it herself. The last thing she needed right now was for her mom to make a big fuss over her.

"Mom, no," Nina said as her mom reached them and began to catch her breath.

"Honey, I just want to make sure you have your things with you—"

"Mom."

"—just in case you need it, I mean wouldn't you rather have it with you? Really honey, sometimes—"

"Mom!" Nina shouted, turning a couple of heads among the other families huddled nearby, then turning them right back with a 360-degree icy glare. "It's fine. We're just going to be a minute. You've got to start letting me take care of myself sometime."

Nina's mom let the bag drop to her side. "I'm sorry, it's just . . ." she started, but instead of finishing she flung herself at Nina and wrapped her in a bear hug. "I just worry sometimes. And this hasn't been the easiest day."

Steve alternated between looking at his shoes and the shoes of everyone around him. Nina slowly gave in and returned her mother's embrace, taking the bag from her. "Mom, it's fine. We'll be right back. You've got nothing to worry about."

CHAPTER 2

"Hey, I'm sorry about your mom," Steve said as soon as Nina's mom had retreated back into the sea of idling evacuees. "I know how you hate that."

Nina shoved the canvas bag into the crook of her arm and walked along the edge of the crowd on the mall side of the parking lot. "Steve, there's a whole lot more that you have to be sorry for," she said.

He followed along after her. "Hey, hold on."

Nina wished she had worn layers. She was starting to get warm, despite the mid-October chill. She ignored Steve and continued on toward the mall's front entrance. She just needed to sit in the shade for a minute, and Steve just needed to leave her alone. She could see where he was coming from, but he never was good at timing.

That had been the problem. As soon as they started dating, he went in full force, and they went from being a will-they-won't-they sort of thing to being basically married.

At least that's how Steve made it seem at school, at home, and pretty much anywhere else where there were other people around. At first it had been kind of cute, but pretty soon she got tired of being *Nina and Steve*, a single unit, instead of just Nina and Steve, who lived down the street from each other and were always hanging out.

The glass on the mall doors felt cool on the back of her head as she leaned up against it in the shade. She pressed the back of her palms against the door, and they left streaks of sweat behind when she took them off.

The sweat. And the irritability, and the uncomfortable too-warm feeling. All the signs.

It had taken her longer than it should have to figure out what was happening, but it always did. To be fair, today had certainly been packed with distractions. But Visitors or no, her blood sugar had been low enough times in her life that she still felt like she should have noticed before her lips started to tingle.

Steve trotted up beside her. "Do you need something?" he offered, snatching her bag of diabetes supplies and clumsily unzipping it.

"Steve, look," she said, "I appreciate it, but I really just need to sit. Can you give my bag back to me?"

"Sure!" He sheepishly handed it back. "Sorry, I just worry about you, babe." When he said the 'b' word a sudden tightness shot through her shoulders, which was definitely not related to low blood sugar.

Nina slid against the glass to sit down and took her test kit out of the pouch. "Please, can we just be quiet for a minute," she said. "Let *me* deal with this."

"Sorry," he said again. "Look, I know this is weird with what happened last night, but . . . I guess I felt like this whole alien invasion kind of changes things."

There was a mechanical click as she pricked her thumb to test her blood sugar. "Yeah Steve, it does—it means there's a lot of stuff we could be worrying about right now other than our relationship status. I mean, this might be the end of the world."

"Right, but that's my point. This might be our last chance to end things on a good note."

Nina pressed the blood onto a test strip, then put it in her meter. She waited for the beep, followed by the bad news, but there was nothing. The Visitor's death ray or EMP or whatever must have fried the thing, but it didn't matter. By now she didn't need the test to tell her what she already knew—she definitely had low blood sugar. "Is this really a good note though?" she asked him.

Steve suddenly became interested in his shoes once more. "Well, maybe they're not here to destroy us," he said. "Maybe they just want to talk. See if we can all get along."

Nina started rummaging in her bag for some glucose tablets. "If that's what they wanted, I doubt they would have made such a dramatic entrance."

"Maybe they just didn't know what else to do," Steve said. He sat down next to her against the doors, though to Nina's relief he managed to keep an appropriate distance. Perhaps he was starting to get the picture. "Maybe they're misunderstood and thought they were running out of time."

She sighed and caught herself starting to feel bad for him again. Actually, she was starting to feel just plain bad, and there weren't any glucose tablets in her bag. "Steve, the problem was never that you aren't sweet enough, and I appreciate the gesture, or whatever this is supposed to be," she said. "But right now, I just really need a soda or something."

"Right," Steve said. "Sorry. Do you think we can make it back to your mom and see if she has anything, or should we check out the mall?"

"If my mom had anything, she would have given it to me when she gave me my supplies. She must not have realized I'm out of glucose tablets," Nina said, thinking about how terrible it would be to pass out or have a seizure in the parking lot in front of everybody.

But maybe they'd all forget when the Visitors came back and annihilated them in the west parking lot of the mall.

"There are some soda machines in the mall," Steve suggested, getting to his feet.

"I don't have any change," Nina said. "And besides, if the buses don't work and my meter doesn't work, what makes you think the soda machines will?"

"I've shaken a few prizes out of a few soda machines in my time. I think I can manage it again." Steve rolled up his sleeves in a mock demonstration of his toughness.

A few months ago Nina would've been amused by his goofiness, but now she just ignored it. Focusing on keeping her balance, she shouldered her bag and slowly stood up while Steve opened one of the doors. She didn't know why she was expecting them to have been locked—the mall had been open earlier this morning.

Regardless, she was relieved to see the doors opened with no trouble. Steve and Nina both stepped into the cavernous, darkened halls of the Oak Grove Mall.

CHAPTER 3

"Wow, it's weird to be in here when it's so empty," Steve said. He and Nina paused just inside the entrance to allow their eyes to adjust. It was mid-afternoon, but inside the mall they may as well have been in the middle of the woods during a lunar eclipse.

Nina's face felt like it was buzzing and she was starting to get dizzy. "Is it? Nobody goes to the mall anymore. You can just buy whatever you want online," she said, brushing him off. She spotted the silhouette of a bench just up ahead and shuffled unsteadily toward it through the darkness, focusing on keeping her balance.

"I suppose. I guess I thought of the mall as,

like, our . . ." Steve trailed off. "Never mind. Hey, I'm gonna go find the soda machines, why don't you just sit tight." He took off without waiting for a response from her. It seemed he'd slipped into a sulky mood, one of his less-than-desirable qualities.

The edge of the bench pinched Nina's knees, but she was too preoccupied with everything else that had gone wrong today to be concerned with the pain. At least it was cool here in the darkness. She couldn't think of another time she'd been glad to be in the mall, other than her first date with Steve a few months back, before everything got so screwed up.

Oh no, she thought to herself. Their first date had been at this mall and clearly the place held some meaning to Steve, and here she was saying that the mall was unimportant. That explained his sudden embarrassment. When he got back, she would make sure to thank him for his help more sincerely than she had outside. He may have been bad with boundaries, and today really wasn't the day to push it, but he'd been trying his best to look after her.

And at least she had Steve with her instead of her mom. He could be kind of a dork sometimes, but at least he wasn't trying to tell her how irresponsible she was for not making sure she had glucose tablets or a snack before leaving the house.

There was a loud series of rattles and clangs in the distance, and before long she spotted a Steve-shaped shadow coming toward her through the darkness. "Here," he said, and she felt the cool condensation of a bottle on one of her shoulders. "Hey, look—" he started, but she cut him off.

"No, hold on," she said. "Thanks for trying to help me today. I know you mean well. Things are just really messed up right now."

She heard him sigh and plop down on the other side of the bench. "Well, I always do," he said.

Nina cracked open the soda with a sticky hiss and took a big gulp. The sweetness hit the back of her throat like a ball of ice laced with molasses and wasps. Orange soda. Chugging sodas or chowing down on candy was never that fun when she had to do it out of desperation, but there were some things she really just couldn't stand, and orange soda was near the top of the list. She didn't want to spit it out, but she felt like she was going to throw up if she didn't. She opened her mouth and let the liquid fall to the floor with a wet smack. "Sorry, Steve, it's just . . . you know how I feel about orange soda." It came off harsher than she'd intended.

"Jeez, Nina, I'm really just trying to help. Do you have to be like that? I can't see in the dark you know. How am I supposed to know what I'm grabbing?"

"No, that's not what I meant—" This time, he was the one who cut her off.

"Hey, I get it, okay? I screw things up. I was screwing things up for the last couple months, and I'm still screwing things up now." He crossed his arms. "It's fine. Look, I gotta take a leak. I think I remember there being a bathroom back there by the vending machines the last time I went to the mall. You know, with you. On our date. Even though nobody goes to the mall anymore, right?"

"Steve," Nina sighed, "I didn't mean it like that. You know I can't think straight when I get low." They were quiet for a moment, and then she turned toward him. "Are you sure you'll be able to find the bathroom in the dark anyway? We should just stay here for a couple of minutes and wait for my blood sugar to go back up, then we can go outside and you can pee in the bushes or whatever." She felt her face flush and cleared her throat. "No one is going to care—the Visitors have everyone a little preoccupied."

The bench shifted as the Steve-shaped shadow stood back up and started to fade back into the darkness. "Yeah, I've already noticed. Aliens are invading and nobody cares about anything else. Look, I need to go for a walk, and if you just have to sit there for a minute anyway, I may as well do it in here."

"Hey, wait a second," Nina called after him, but he was already gone. She sipped on her orange soda. It tasted awful, but it was better than having a full-blown medical emergency.

Over the last few months, this situation had become all too familiar. Nina and Steve never used to have misunderstandings, but ever since they'd started dating, it seemed to happen all the time. Little disagreements that wouldn't have mattered when they were friends had become major problems once they were boyfriend and girlfriend. It was like they couldn't even talk to each other anymore without somehow getting on each other's nerves. And now today was following the same pattern—both of them upset, sulking, trying to pinpoint where it all went wrong. Sure, today the Visitors were here, which made everything worse, but it probably would have gone basically the same way if they would have been sitting in the lunchroom.

Nina was finally starting to feel a little better, but she wanted to give Steve a minute to collect himself. She decided to peek out front to see if the guardsmen had made any progress on the buses. She walked toward the light streaming in through the glass entranceway, feeling herself get a little steadier on her feet as she went. Terrible as it was, the orange soda was doing the trick.

The glare from outside was painful at first, but soon her eyes readjusted to the brightness. She rubbed at her eyes with the heel of her palms. Once her vision began to clear, it wasn't what she saw that alarmed her. It was what she didn't see. The mass of people who had been milling about near the buses just a few minutes ago had vanished. Worse yet, Nina had no idea where they had gone.

CHAPTER 4

Apparently something had made the group decide to give up on the buses. Nina's parents must have figured she was somewhere else in the crowd with Steve and that they could find her later. After all, why would she leave the safety of the group? She had plenty of answers to that question, but they didn't help her now.

Nina tried to estimate how long she and Steve had been inside the mall. It was hard to guess without being able to check the clock on her phone, but she figured it had to be less than fifteen minutes. The group couldn't have gone very far. She could probably start running and catch up to them before they got too much farther away.

But she had no idea which way they had gone. Nina burst out into the parking lot anyway and scanned the distance in every direction, but there was no sign of life. Just the Visitor's ship, hanging over the horizon like the memory of a nightmare.

She wracked her brain, trying to remember if she'd heard the guardsmen say anything about where they would be headed. But between the alien invasion and Steve's insistence on discussing their relationship problems, she hadn't been paying enough attention to overhear anything useful.

But one thing seemed obvious: if everyone else had left, there had to be a good reason. It probably wasn't safe to be here—especially in the parking lot, stationary and out in the open. Nina retreated back inside, swallowing a wave of fear for her parents. She desperately hoped they were okay. But for the moment she had to focus on keeping herself safe. All her life she'd heard stories about the mall being originally built as a bomb shelter. Those were probably just rumors, but any sturdy structure was probably safer than the unprotected parking lot. And besides, she couldn't just leave Steve here by himself with no way of knowing what happened to her or the others.

Back inside the mall, Nina shuffled back toward the bench where she had been resting as her eyes slowly readjusted to the darkness. Once she filled Steve in, they'd figure out how to try to find everyone else. Or maybe someone would come back for them once their parents noticed they weren't with the group.

"Steve!" she called out. No answer. "Steve! Everyone is leaving—you need to come out." Again, the almost pitch-black hallway offered no answer in return.

Steve was probably back there letting her stew. In the past few months, she'd learned that he was a master of weaponizing silence. Nina felt around and found the empty soda bottle she had left on the bench. She tossed the bottle into the darkness, toward where she thought Steve must be. A moment later she heard it clatter and skid, echoing down the hallway. That should get his attention.

She waited.

"Steve!" she tried again.

It became clear that this wasn't working, so Nina decided she would have to go after him. She edged her way over to one side of the corridor, figuring that she could feel her way along the wall until she came to the area with the soda machines, supposed bathroom, and—hopefully—Steve. Keeping one hand flat against the wall, she cautiously began to move deeper into the mall. There were plenty of things to bump into in the darkness.

The flat, smooth wall quickly gave way to the cool glass of display windows, alternating with the ribbed metal of the security fencing that still covered most of the stores' entrances. She managed to make it past two storefronts when she heard a plastic sort of scraping sound up ahead of her.

"Steve!" Nina stopped, pressed up against a window display. "Steve, is that you?"

There was a strained grunt up ahead. Nina tried to scan farther ahead, but she couldn't make anything out other than dancing shadows and vague outlines of unknown objects in the near total darkness before her. She wondered if the Visitors were already in the mall with them—and if Steve was okay. He could be difficult sometimes, but he wouldn't keep up with something like this just because he was mad at her. A shadow danced out of the corner of her eye through the display window. Nina held her breath and peered through the glass, trying to make out what might be hiding in the store. Slowly, a form began to take shape.

Nina gasped and fell backward, feeling her heart stop. The form was human-shaped but hunched over, legs splayed impossibly wide. Its face was almost right up against the glass, and it had bizarre protrusions coming out of its back and head.

"Steve, I need your help!" she choked out and began crawling backward away from the window.

Several dull, wet thuds came from just up ahead all at once, followed by the heavy footfalls of somebody running. "Nina, hang on!" Steve called out. Nina looked toward the sound of his voice and thought she saw Steve's silhouette coming toward her in the darkness farther down the hall.

There was a loud crunch and then another scraping sound. Steve screamed, and then Nina couldn't focus on anything but trying to get her breath back as one of Steve's bony elbows crashed into her stomach, knocking the wind out of her. He'd managed to trip over the bottle she'd thrown into the darkness earlier while running full speed. She struggled to suck in air as Steve scrambled to disentangle himself from her.

Steve groaned loudly in pain as he collected himself, then asked, "Are you all right? What happened?"

Between gasping breaths, Nina managed to tell him, "In the window . . . something in the window . . . like a human but not right." She swallowed heavily. "The Visitors . . . things sticking out of its head and back."

Steve groaned again, but this time there was a little bit of frustration mixed in with pain. "Something in the window of a mall that looks like a human but not quite right . . . like a mannequin wearing a hat and a backpack?" he asked, then started to chuckle. "Jeez Nina, I didn't know you were still scared of the dark."

She felt her face getting hot again, but this time it wasn't because of a medical emergency. "Hey, shut up—today is not a normal day. Why weren't you answering me? And why don't you watch where you're going?"

They pulled themselves to their feet, each rubbing at their fresh bruises. "I was getting you some more sodas for the road," he explained. "I figured that if I grabbed as many as I could there were bound to be a couple in there that weren't orange. And," he paused, clearing his throat, "I may have tried to hold an extra one between my teeth."

From what little she could see, Nina couldn't make out any bottles in his arms. "So, where are they?"

"I had trouble keeping hold of everything once I heard you were in trouble, but it got even harder when I was flying through the air," Steve said. "As to watching where I'm going,

I don't have night vision. Besides, I didn't want to see anything scary."

"You are a huge dork," she said. It was nice to laugh, but she knew they didn't have much time to waste. "But listen. Everybody else is gone—they must have decided to abandon the buses. We have to try to catch up with them, and I wouldn't mind getting out of this mall."

She couldn't see his face in the darkness, but his voice was deadly serious. "All right, we gotta go then."

They turned and hurried toward the light of the entryway in the distance. About halfway there, they heard a deafening crash as the glass on one of the doors shattered. A hulking figure appeared and started to climb into the mall through the broken door.

CHAPTER 5

They weren't able to see the figure clearly because of the bright light streaming in through the broken glass behind it. Despite the recent beating he'd taken stumbling around in the darkness, Steve didn't waste any time jumping between Nina and the unknown intruder—which may or may not be an alien. "Stay back!" he shouted, attempting to look bigger than he was by puffing out his shoulders.

The darkened silhouette paused midway through the shattered window. Encouraged that he was having any effect at all, Steve took another step forward and continued shouting at the monster. "That's right, alien scum. If you wanna get to her, you're going to have to go through me!"

Nina wondered if that was as embarrassing for Steve to say as it was for her to hear. When they were kids, he'd never really bought into all the macho nonsense, but to Nina's dismay lately he'd started growing into it. "Steve," she hissed. "Let's go! What are you going to do, fight this thing? It's gotta be twice your size! And it's from *space!*"

She could see his shoulders deflate a little bit at her suggestion, but then the figure retreated slightly back through the door frame, which emboldened Steve further. "*Shhh*, I think it's working!" he hissed back over his shoulder, then turned to face the beast. "That's right, there's nothing for you in here! Get out! Skedaddle!"

The figure spread its arms out wide and began running them along the edges of the doorframe, sending the remaining fragments of the window tinkling to the ground. Then it went back to pressing itself forward, although now it seemed to be caught on the doorframe by a large hump on its back.

"*Skedaddle?*" Nina hissed. "Seriously, Steve? Let's just get out of here while we still can."

If Steve really wanted to impress her, he could have tried a little harder to make sure he'd survive the next five minutes instead of swaggering at a monster from outer space that likely didn't understand English.

The alien was making strained grunts now, stretched forward as it forced its body through the doorframe. It was making headway.

"Save yourself, Nina!" Steve called back over his shoulder. "I'll buy you some time."

Nina was becoming less frightened and more frustrated by the moment. The Visitor was being thwarted pretty handily by an unlocked glass door, and Steve seemed to have switched his brain into some other mode that thought only in action star one-liners.

"Steve," she said, trying to keep her voice even and calm, "I really don't think that's necessary. I think we both should just get out of here." She placed a hand on his shoulder, causing him to jerk sharply in surprise. "This thing looks pretty busy with that door. Let's just run across the mall and bolt out the other side."

She felt his shoulders relax as she left her hand gently resting on his arm. Steve rapidly looked back and forth between her and the doorway. The Visitor was almost through the door, but the struggle seemed to be taking a lot out of it. Now that Steve had stopped shouting at it for a moment, it seemed to have completely stopped focusing on them.

"Okay," he said. "Good plan."

They slowly backed up into the darkness, trying not make any sudden moves that could draw the creature's attention again. But they hadn't gone more than a few steps before the struggling mass in the doorway paused again and the mall fell into an uneasy silence.

"Hey!" The Visitor shouted at them, sounding much more human than either of them expected it to. "Wait a second, I'm stuck in the door!"

CHAPTER 6

Nina and Steve paused and exchanged glances in the darkness. Steve put a finger to his lips and Nina nodded her agreement. It could be a trick.

"Come on, wait up! You can't leave me out here to die!" the Visitor called out. "Steve, is that you back there? I thought I heard you yelling."

The voice sounded familiar, but Nina couldn't quite place it. In the back of her memory she could hear the same voice calling out, steadier and deeper from the window of a moving car last summer.

"Come on you nerd, I know you're not gonna let them take me!" That was it. Nina placed him as soon as she heard 'nerd.'

". . . Jack Kurten?" Nina called cautiously.

"Yeah, now get me out of this doorway before the aliens come back!"

"Great," Steve mumbled, then ran toward the door. Nina walked along after him. By the time she caught up, Steve had managed to disentangle Jack's backpack from the doorframe and help him to his feet.

He was a sight to see. Jack Kurten was six-foot-five and looked at least half as wide, especially wrapped in his bulky letterman jacket. He lifted a large hand and brushed broken glass out of his hair.

"Hi, Jack," Nina said impatiently. If she could've chosen someone else to get stuck with during the possible end of the world, Jack wouldn't have been her top pick. Still, it was a relief to know that she and Steve weren't completely alone.

Jack shouldered his backpack, which he'd had to remove to get through the door. "Well, well, well," he said. "So aliens invade and Nina and Steve set up a freaking love nest at the Oak

Grove Mall. You guys are really too cute to live, you know that?"

Steve glanced at Nina with a pained look on his face. Nina gave him a slight shake of her head. Considering everything else that was happening, she didn't feel the need to explain to Jack that they were no longer a couple. "Nina's blood sugar got low," Steve said. "We had to get her something."

"Well, you guys got lucky. The National Guard had us hoofing it to some shelter, then we saw another one of those ships, but smaller—and this time it landed. Those soldiers told us to get down and started setting up like they were gonna have a shoot-out with the aliens." He coughed. "I was right there with them, but I didn't want to get stuck in a laser fight with nothing but my fists, you know?"

"So what happened?" Steve asked.

"I don't know," Jack said. "It was really confusing, all right? I don't know what happened after that."

Nina stared at him. "What do you mean you don't know?" Her mind was racing. The

Visitors might have taken the rest of the group hostage, or worse.

Jack brushed the last bits of shattered glass out of his hair. "Oh, like you guys would have stuck around for that," he snapped.

"Wait a minute," Steve said. "You just *left?*"

Jack glared at him. "I know you're probably into aliens, being Weird Steve and all, but I don't need to mess around with space monsters. I don't think you do either, even if you're pretty good at talking a big game in front of your little girlfriend."

"Hey!" Steve said, starting to tense up again.

Nina held up her hands. "Guys, c'mon. Let's not get into this right now. Jack, what happened to everyone else? Do you know where you guys were going when the Visitors attacked?"

"No, I was just following the crowd. I don't even know if those soldier guys actually had much of a plan—it seemed like they were arguing with each other," Jack said. He glanced quickly out the door, then returned his attention to the others. "You guys weren't there. You don't get it. I figured I could come back here and get my car started while they were distracted with everybody else. Maybe I could . . . I don't know."

Steve scoffed. "You're a real hero, Jack."

Nina half expected Jack to haul Steve off and knock his teeth out, and for a second it looked like he was going to. But then he just sighed and snapped, "Yeah Steve, just like you. I'm sure if you'd been there you would've been able to scare them off. Get real. You wouldn't have lasted two seconds out there."

There was an uncomfortable moment of silence. Nina realized they had no way of knowing what had happened to their families. Steve took another step away from them and gave the doorframe a solid kick. He must have been having the same thought.

Jack shook his head back and forth and then pulled one of his hands backward through his hair. By the time he returned his arm to his side, he seemed to have shaken it off.

"Whatever. It's just whatever," Jack said. "So what's the plan here? Or have you been too busy making out in here to come up with anything good?"

Nina felt heat start to build up in her cheekbones and knew she must be turning bright red. It took everything she had to ignore the comment. Luckily, Steve barely seemed to register what Jack had said. "No, we haven't come up with a plan yet. We've been stuck in here, so we didn't know how bad it had gotten out there."

Jack began pacing back and forth. Steve watched with his arms crossed and an eyebrow arched. Nina wondered how long he would give Jack before making a snarky comment.

Then, out of nowhere, Steve bolted away from the doors. Before Jack and Nina could ask what he was doing, he began loudly shushing them and gesturing for them to back away from the entrance.

They retreated several yards into the darkness before Nina grabbed hold of Steve to stop him. "Steve, what is it?"

"Something's out there," he said, voice shaking. "I saw it slip between the buses."

Jack crouched beside them. "What was it?" he asked.

"I don't know, but I don't want to find out," Steve hissed.

"Well neither do I," Jack said. "I was just out there—it's not great."

Nina sat back, briefly considering their options. Since this invasion had started they'd been both literally and figuratively in the dark, and they didn't have much to show for it other than perhaps lasting slightly longer before getting abducted. If they didn't figure out what was going on in the parking lot, they'd probably just end up sitting there, half-in, half-out of the mall. Eventually they would either be captured where they sat, or her blood sugar would get low again and they'd have to move without having any idea what their options were.

"I'm going to check it out," she said.

"No!" both boys said in unison. But she had already started crawling back toward the doorway. She'd had enough of discussion for the moment. It was time to get something done.

CHAPTER 7

Nina crept toward the exit. Once she got closer to the doors, she carefully avoided the broken glass that littered the floor. She positioned herself in the lower corner of the door farthest from the broken one. She cautiously scanned the parking lot. Other than the lack of people and the pair of jeeps the guardsmen had left behind, everything outside appeared astonishingly normal. The sun was even out. She reminded herself not to slip into a false sense of security and focused intently on the line of buses in the center of the lot.

It would have helped if she had any idea what she was actually looking for. So far they'd only ever seen the Visitors' ships—she had no idea what the aliens themselves looked like.

She thought about different types of aliens she'd seen in all the movies Steve used to make her watch. Based on that, she was either looking for something pretty large, maybe a little bigger than Jack, or else something normal-sized but with a giant head.

Still, it was possible they could change their shape. She wondered briefly if Jack was really who he said he was. Could he actually be an alien disguised to look like Jack Kurten? But she quickly dismissed the idea. Jack had trouble doing basic human things like getting through a door, but that was also standard Jack. Plus, if Jack were a shapeshifter, he wouldn't have called Steve "Weird Steve" or known that Nina had been dating him.

A sudden movement near the buses interrupted her thoughts. She inched closer to the door and peered through it, practically pressing her nose up against the glass. There it was again. A flicker of light was coming from behind the front tires of one of the buses.

Slowly, a helmeted human head poked out. It was one of the guardsmen from earlier— he must have somehow made it back to the mall. He reached an arm out and began manipulating what she could now see was a small mirror. He flashed reflected sunlight toward her in regular intervals. The broken glass behind her crunched underfoot, and then a hand grabbed her shoulder and startled her.

"Don't do that!" she hissed at Steve, who had crept up behind her as she had been observing the parking lot.

"I think he's trying to signal us," he said. "It might be Morse code."

Nina shifted her weight so she could glare at Steve. "Great, so do you know Morse code?"

He shook his head.

"Well then that's not very much help, is it," she sighed. "I'm going to see if I can get him to come over here."

She slowly lifted herself up and waved to the guardsman, who continued flashing the mirror at them. She mouthed that she couldn't understand and then began waving him toward them. He dropped the mirror and shook his head, then returned the same gesture she'd been giving him, urging them to come join him outside. She looked at Steve, who was shaking his head.

"You heard what Jack said—we're not going out there," he told her.

The guardsman was standing up now, no longer trying to conceal himself with the bus, and frantically waving at them. There was a flash of movement in the sky above him, and Nina could see one of the smaller Visitor ships approaching. Nina pounded on the glass, trying to draw the soldier's attention to the ship. The guard spotted it and took off, sprinting back toward the woods.

"We have to get out of here—now!" Steve shouted. "Before they see us!"

Nina was rooted in place. *If the soldier came back here alone*, she wondered, *what does that mean for the others?*

"Nina! Come on! Get up!" Steve urged, grabbing her by the shoulder. "It's getting closer!"

The ship seemed to crawl through the sky as it passed the mall and continued in the direction the soldier went. Nina snapped back into action and pushed herself up off the floor, catching a shard of glass with her palm in her rush to get away from the windows and opening up a deep gash. As they hurried back into the darkness, she couldn't help but wonder what would happen to the soldier.

CHAPTER 8

In their rush to get away from the windows, they almost ran into Jack.

"Hey, wait a second—slow down," he said. "What happened?"

Nina only slowed enough to grab him by the shoulder and drag him deeper into the mall. "They're out there, and they're headed this way!" she shouted. "There was a soldier, but I think . . . he's gone now."

She didn't have to tell Jack twice. The trio barreled on through the darkness, banging shins and kneecaps against benches and planters as they went. The blood was sticky and hot on Nina's palm, but at least the cut didn't hurt. She wondered how bad it was, but there was no way to tell without any light. They pressed onward, deeper into the mall until they lost sight of the entryway. Nina's arm was starting to feel strange—a little lighter than it should and cold and tingly just underneath the skin, like it was falling asleep.

"Hold it!" she called out. The group stopped, loudly catching their breaths. "This isn't going to work—we need a plan."

"Hang on," Jack said. Nina heard Jack's backpack hit the ground with a heavy thud, followed by a zipper and the sound of him rummaging through the pack. "Okay, everybody stand back to back."

"Why?" Steve asked.

There was a grunt off to Nina's left. "Just do it, all right?" Jack said.

After groping in the darkness to find one another, the group assembled back to back, facing outward. There was a loud crack like the striking of a match, and suddenly Nina's nostrils burned with the rotten egg stench of sulfur. The area around them was illuminated with a flickering light, and she turned around to see that Jack was holding a road flare.

"Ugh, that smells awful," she said, suppressing a sneeze from the sting in her nose.

"It's the sulfur in the flare," Steve said. He turned beside her, the light dancing across his sweat-smeared forehead. "Where did you even get that? Did you have that the whole time?"

Jack grinned. "I dumped my books when I heard about the space ships and got some stuff out of the safety kit I keep in my car," he explained. "I figure it's more likely to do me some good than a bunch of homework, given the situation."

"That's . . . surprisingly good thinking, Jack. What else do you—" Steve started, but Jack interrupted him with a sharp gasp.

"Nina, what happened to your hand?"

Nina glanced down at her palm. It looked pretty bad. Her whole hand was red and sticky with blood, and it had dripped all over her shirt and pants during their retreat into the mall.

"Whoa, Nina," Steve stammered. "What happened? Are you okay?"

Nina's arm was still tingling. She hadn't realized how bad her injury actually was. She took a deep gulp of air in attempt to push down the panic that was rising up in her chest. "I cut myself on the glass," she said. "I didn't think it was that bad."

"Umm, you're looking at your hand, right?" Jack said sarcastically. "It's really bad."

"Thanks, Jack, really helpful," barked Steve. "We gotta find something to stop the bleeding—a T-shirt or something." He glanced around the illuminated circle provided by the road flare. "There!" He pointing to a storefront whose security fencing wasn't quite closed.

"I cut myself on the glass," Nina felt herself saying again. She was starting to feel strange, like none of this was actually happening, and she was just in somebody else's bad dream.

"You're gonna be okay," Steve told her. "Just hang in there. Jack, help me with this."

Jack set down the road flare. Then he and Steve grabbed onto the bottom of the fencing and forced it open, grunting with the effort. After retrieving the flare, Jack and Steve slid under the gate and into the store, beckoning for Nina to follow. She did clumsily, leaving a trail of blood droplets in her wake.

They were in some kind of novelty shop, full of various odds and ends, party supplies, and T-shirts with bad one-liners and edgy slogans plastered across the front. Steve rushed over to a rack of shirts and tried to tear one into strips. The shirt proved surprisingly strong, and if they weren't already in such a bad situation, it would have been pretty embarrassing.

"Seriously, Steve?" Jack said, grabbing another shirt from the pile and taking it apart at the seams with ease.

"I didn't think it was that bad," Nina said, still dripping blood onto the floor steadily. She felt as if there was something that she really needed to do, but couldn't remember what it was. She looked at the sticky mess that was her hand. *I should probably take care of that*, she thought to herself in a daze.

Steve grabbed the strips out of Jacks hands and began winding them tightly around Nina's hand, applying pressure to the wound. "Here, it's okay. Just sit," he told her, helping her to the ground. "We'll just sit here for a while, and you'll be fine." Nina started to shiver all over, suddenly feeling freezing cold.

"It's cold," she mumbled. "I cut my hand on the glass. I didn't think it was that bad."

Steve grabbed a hoodie and wrapped it around her shoulders. "You're all right, you're all right," he reassured her, then turned to Jack. "Hey, we gotta rest here for a minute. Why don't you look around and see if you can find anything useful in here."

Jack nodded and disappeared into the racks of novelty items.

Steve grabbed her hand with both hands and held it above her head. "Let's just keep this elevated so the bleeding slows down."

This is nice, Nina thought, although the voice in her head sounded like it was coming from a million miles away. Her brain felt like it was wading through molasses. *Sitting feels nice. We'll just sit for a while.* She looked over at Steve. *It's nice that he's trying so hard.*

"I'm sorry," she said then. "I didn't think it was that bad."

He looked her in the eye and squeezed her hand even tighter between his. "Don't worry," he told her. "It's not. Everything is going to be okay."

CHAPTER 9

By the light of the road flare, Jack searched
the store for anything that might help them
survive while Steve continued applying
pressure to Nina's wound. It took a while, but
eventually the bleeding stopped. Nina started
to feel a little more like herself, although she
was a little lightheaded. Still, she didn't want to
stay in the store any longer than they had to.
In the time they'd spent collecting themselves,
it was entirely possible that the Visitors had
somehow detected their presence and entered
the mall. She didn't want to wait in one spot
and find out.

She tried to pull her hand away from
Steve's, but he wasn't paying attention and his

hands wouldn't seem to let go. Nina cleared her throat and gave another gentle but sturdy tug. "Steve, you can, uh, stop holding my hand," she said.

"Oh, sorry," he responded sheepishly, checking her makeshift bandages one last time before letting go. "We should try to find some real bandages and some antibiotics or something," he said. "You don't want it to get infected."

Nina snorted. "If we live that long."

"It just seems like a good idea," Steve said. "We might as well try to stay positive."

Jack returned with his haul, looking pleased with himself. "All right, I think I found some good stuff. I got a bunch of glow sticks, some more T-shirts in case any of you klutzes manage to hurt yourselves again, some kind of weird samurai-looking sword thing . . ." He swung a model katana into a mug, shattering it instantly. "And two hundred fifty bucks!"

"Hey, be careful with that sword!" Steve cried as he stepped away from the pieces of the shattered mug on the floor. "What is it with you and breaking things?"

"What is it with you and not knowing how to just chill?" Jack retorted. His road flare began to sputter in his hand, and it fizzled out by the time Steve came up with an answer.

"It's a little hard to chill when everyone we know might've just been abducted by aliens!"

"Thanks, man, I definitely forgot about that." Jack dropped the dead flare, cracked a glow stick, and handed some more to Steve and Nina. They didn't offer as much light as the road flare, and definitely lacked its intimidation factor, but at least they smelled better.

Despite her recent injury, Nina had other concerns. "Did you say you found two hundred fifty dollars?"

"It was in the register." Jack grinned. "Don't worry, I'll share."

"You can keep it. I don't want to go to jail when this is over," Steve grumbled.

Nina looked at Jack sternly. "I think you should leave the money where you found it, Jack. Besides, I doubt the Visitors take cash."

"You guys really are nerds," Jack laughed.

"But fine, whatever, we'll leave the money."
He tossed the bills over his shoulder and
they rained down among the merchandise,
illuminated by the blue and green light of the
glow sticks. "So what now?" he asked.

"I think I saw a directory out there," Steve
said. "We should figure out what's around
so we can plan our next move." Although he
had been irritating at first, Nina was actually
starting to appreciate crisis-mode Steve. He was
surprisingly good at this, and he was certainly
a lot less sulky than postbreakup Steve.

The group gathered up their supplies in
Jack's backpack and cautiously slid back out
under the storefront fencing, keeping their
eyes and ears open for any sign of the Visitors.
It didn't take them long to find the directory,
and they surveyed the listings in search of
anything useful.

"So, I don't want to be a whiner," Jack
started. "But Coach has us doing two-a-days,
so I've been doubling up on the protein in the
mornings lately, but with the whole green-
men-from-outer-space situation I didn't get my

hands on any grub yet today. I'm thinking we hit the food court." He turned to Nina. "Don't you have some kind of disease where you're addicted to sugar? We could probably grab something for you there."

Steve turned to Jack with a scowl and said, "Has anyone ever told you that you've got a real problem with how you talk to people?"

Jack laughed and mussed Steve's hair. "Nobody who's lived to tell the tale, Stevie."

Nina ignored them, studying the map intensely. It wasn't listed in the directory, but on the map itself there was a room near the YOU ARE HERE arrow that was labeled SYSTEMS AND MAINTENANCE.

Steve had managed to pull away from Jack and now the two were locked in a sort of standoff. "Hey, can you guys grow up for a second?" Nina said. "I've got a plan." She told them about the systems and maintenance room. "People always say this place was originally supposed to be a bomb shelter. And even if that's not the case, this is definitely an old building with thick walls. Maybe the

EMP didn't penetrate all the way through the building. That room might have some electronics that aren't fried—maybe even a way to get some power back on."

"That's great, Nina," Steve said. "But I really think we should get you something for your hand, and there's a pharmacy in the next wing. We could head over there and get some bandages and disinfectant. I'll bet they've got some insulin and glucose tabs too."

Jack groaned. "I know I'm gonna get outvoted on this one 'cause you two are in love with each other or whatever, but could we *please* grab something to eat first?"

Steve winced. "I don't really care about your stomach right now, Jack. Besides, I'm sure there are snacks at the pharmacy."

Nina decided that, for everyone's sake, she may as well let Jack in on the fact that they weren't together anymore. The last thing Steve needed right now was Jack constantly twisting the knife. "First of all," she started, "Steve and I broke up, so I'd appreciate it if you could shut up about it." Jack started to say something, but Nina silenced him with an icy glare. "Second, as touched as I am by all this concern for my 'sugar addiction,' everything is gonna be a whole lot easier if we can get some lights on, or at least some working flashlights."

The boys shuffled their feet and looked at each other. Jack raised an arm and Steve winced in anticipation, but Jack was just moving to clap him on the back. "Sorry man, I know it can be rough with girls. You'll get used to it once you've had more than one girlfriend. Don't lose hope."

Steve ignored him. "Nina's right. These glow sticks are great and everything, but it would probably be better if we had something with a little more oomph to it."

"Fine," Jack grunted. "Let's go then, I guess. But after this, we're getting some snacks."

CHAPTER 10

On the way to the systems and maintenance room, the group began to hear strange noises from elsewhere in the mall. At first nobody said anything about it, but soon the sounds were getting closer.

"You guys hear that?" Jack whispered.

"Yes, now shut up!" Nina hissed back.

Steve glanced uneasily at the walls and then at the ceiling. "I've seen this before in movies," he whispered. "I think they're in the walls."

"You think it's the Visitors?" Nina asked.

The group halted and waited for a moment, listening intently. Nina peered into the darkness at the edge of the glow sticks' range. The door to Systems and Maintenance should be somewhere right around here. She spotted the door frame just as another alien sound echoed through the cavernous hallway, although this time it seemed to be a little farther away. It sounded like there were several voices, completely inhuman. *Okay*, she thought, *that's* definitely *the Visitors*. Judging by the back-and-forth of the voices, they seemed to be communicating with one another.

Nina gestured for the boys to follow her and they hurried on toward the doorway. Once they were all in position next to the door, they waited. Nina glanced at the boys and placed a finger to her lips.

The sounds faded into the distance. It was starting to seem like they might make it out of this after all, or at least manage to stay safe for a little while longer. Soon the mall fell silent once more. Steve pointed to Jack, then held up a fist and pointed toward the door, then pointed to himself before indicating the door handle. Nina exchanged glances with both of them, then held up a handful of glow sticks. Jack nodded and positioned himself in front of the door, setting down his backpack and gripping the replica samurai sword like a baseball bat. Steve eased himself alongside the door then got a grip on its handle. Nina crouched on the other side of the doorframe and cracked the glows sticks. She met the others' eyes and then counted down from five with her fingers.

On one, Jack let out a roar and swung the replica sword. At the same time Steve wrenched the door handle and attempted to throw it open, but it was locked. There was a loud pop as his shoulder slipped out of its socket. Between the angle and the adrenaline, he'd been positioned perfectly wrong for any resistance from the door. He fell to the ground with a pained yelp. A split second later Jack's sword struck the wall where Steve had just been, shattering on contact and sending bits of metal flying in all directions. Meanwhile, Nina had already tossed the glow sticks toward what should have been an open door. They bounced off and fell harmlessly to the floor.

"Ugh, my arm," Steve groaned. "I think there's something wrong with it."

Nina glanced over. Steve's arm was stuck at an impossible angle, dangling from his shoulder. "Just don't look at it," she said.

Jack rubbed his hands together. Nina realized they must be stinging from striking the wall with the sword so hard. "Yeah man, it's probably not as bad as it looks."

That was the wrong thing to say. Steve twisted himself around to face the glow sticks and see the damage for himself. Once he saw the arm, his groans turned to a panicked scream.

Nina quickly knelt at his side and began shushing him. "I know it hurts, but you're going to have to be quiet here, all right? They might hear you and come back."

"Nina's right," Jack whispered. "Don't worry, I've dealt with this before. Guys get their shoulders dislocated all the time out on the field."

"I guess sports really are good for something after all," Steve groaned.

Jack smirked. "I'd watch that mouth of yours, Steve. In my experience this can be quite painful. Now lie on your back—I'm gonna grab your arm and pull it gently away from you. You brace yourself against my chest, and that should pop it back into place. We're gonna want to get a sling on it afterward though. I'd hate to see your career as a quarterback end before it has the chance to start."

A moment later Steve's shoulder popped back in with a sickening clunk. Once the maneuver was done, Jack tore up another T-shirt, tying it into a makeshift sling. "There we have it, and you didn't even cry. You're impressing me today, Stevie."

"Jack, can you please stop being a jerk for ten seconds here?" Nina whispered. "We still have to get this door open."

Just then, the trio heard a strange clicking and rattling from behind the door. They froze in terror and watched helplessly as the handle began to turn.

CHAPTER 11

The door slid open with the excruciating shriek of unoiled hinges. A figure towered above them, framed in an eerie orange glow. It looked part human and part machine. Its torso was covered in some sort of futuristic plastic armor, and its face was hidden by a thick black visor.

Jack snatched up a handful of glow sticks that Nina had thrown at the door a moment ago. He cracked them open, allowing the group to get a better look at the cosmic terror they were about to face.

The creature removed one of its oversized hands, revealing something shockingly similar to a human hand underneath its boxy exterior. Nina, Steve, and Jack remained motionless, stunned into silence. Then the creature reached up and removed its helmet, exposing the face of a red-haired teenage girl.

"Hey, I know you!" Jack said. "You're that weird chick who was always reading lawn mower manuals and stuff at school. I thought you graduated."

Nina recognized her too. Alexa Carmichael was a couple years ahead of them in school. She'd usually kept to herself. Nina was surprised to see her in the mall—she'd always assumed Alexa would be at MIT or something by now.

"Oh," Alexa said. "I thought you might be the aliens. I was hoping to join them. I guess you'll have to do. Come in then." She reached behind the doorframe, pulled out a working flashlight, and beckoned for them to follow her.

The group scrambled to their feet and entered the systems and maintenance room. Nina made a point of slamming the door shut behind them and locking it.

"As you can see, the electronics in here didn't get fried along with everything else,"

Alexa said. "I'm sure you've heard that the mall was built to be a bomb shelter. That's not strictly true, but this part of the mall was. Now we just use it for maintenance."

"What do you mean we?" Nina asked. "Do you work here or something?"

The hallway they were walking down opened up to a larger room. The walls were lined with shelves containing tools, batteries, cleaning supplies, and other odds and ends. Near the back of the room there was a wide freight elevator with its cage closed. On a table against the wall, Alexa had set up a flashlight as light source, with several batteries charging next to it. A few folding chairs were set up haphazardly around the table.

"Well, I don't work maintenance—I work at Pretzel Boss," Alexa clarified. "I'm an assistant manager, but I think a promotion may be just around the corner . . . or was anyway," she sighed. "After today's complication, I'm not sure I have much of a future with Pretzel Boss."

Jack grabbed one of the chairs and flipped it around so he could straddle it, folding his arms over its back. "But what are you doing here? I thought you were a genius or something. I would've figured you'd gotten out of this town. I mean, even if you didn't before, I don't know why you'd stay now, what with the aliens and everything."

Alexa took a seat, and Nina and Steve found chairs of their own as well. "I got some scholarships, yes," Alexa said, "but it was all just so depressing. Everyone else was going to college to be with their friends, ready to have the time of their lives. Everybody expects me to go off on my own and be a hermit and build a better mouse trap or maybe solve cold fusion."

"What's wrong with that? Isn't that, like, your thing anyway?" Steve asked. The pain in his arm appeared to be subsiding, although he still winced a little whenever he moved it.

"Yes, it is," Alexa said. "But that wouldn't have been very surprising at all, would it? When I graduated, I realized I'd never done anything surprising in my life. I never really even got to know anyone here. I said to myself,

'What would be more surprising than taking a job at the mall? Maybe I'll even make friends with a few of my coworkers.'"

Jack scratched his head. "So, uh, how's that working out for you?"

"Not so well," Alexa said. "But at least it was surprising. You all, though . . . you are quite surprising. I think the real question is what are *you* doing here? Shouldn't you have run off with the rest of the town?"

Nina explained their situation—how they had become trapped in the mall, pursued by unknown creatures and contending with injuries, and how now they were hoping to get the power back on, gather supplies, and plan their next move.

"How exciting!" Alexa said.

"Not the word I would use," said Nina dryly.

"Well, as luck would have it, there's a backup generator back here, down in the subbasement," Alexa said. "And as far as I know, it should still work—the concrete walls of this mall are very thick, and this deep underground, nothing seems to have been disrupted by the EMP. There's a chance that some of the light fixtures, the concrete ones anyway, survived as well."

Nina felt a wave of relief—quickly followed by suspicion. This seemed a little too good to be true. And was she really supposed to buy that Alexa basically threw away her whole future just because she didn't have many friends and her life wasn't surprising enough? "Hang on," Nina said. "I'm still confused. You explained why you're here, but what about why you're here *today*?"

Alexa stood up and walked over to the table, picking up one of the flashlights and flicking it on, then began pacing around the room as she explained. "You're probably wondering why I'm dressed this way too. As I said, things at Pretzel Boss aren't great. My coworkers also aren't that clever." She sighed and let out a bitter laugh.

"I'm the only one who can fix the nacho cheese machine, which breaks every two weeks or so. Today is my unlucky day, I guess. I caught the broadcast about the Visitors while

I was doing some early morning maintenance. I realized that this could be my big chance. A chance to make contact with extraterrestrial life. While everybody else is running around shooting at them, or each other, I might be able to actually communicate with alien life forms, maybe even take a look at some of their technology."

"That's . . . wow. Not the way I reacted to this situation," Steve said.

"Yeah, I'm with Steve on this one," Jack chimed in.

Nina shot them both a glare for their rudeness but didn't really disagree with them. All in all, for a smart girl, Alexa seemed to make some pretty strange decisions. Then again, high school wasn't easy for anybody. Nina knew she couldn't claim that *she'd* made all the right choices.

"You think the Visitors came here to recruit new talent for their tech industry?" said Steve, his tone a blend of sarcasm and outrage. "You think they're looking for some plucky human sidekick to share their secrets with?"

Alexa flushed. "Maybe not. But I think it's worthwhile to keep an open mind. And I did take *some* precautions—I got some protection from one of the sporting goods stores." She tapped her plastic armor, which in the light they could now see was adorned with a motocross logo. "I decided to come back here and wait for things to calm down a bit before attempting to make contact. This early on there are bound to be . . . misunderstandings."

Jack stood up, knocking over his chair as he did so. "Well, understand me—those aliens have already hunted down everyone else we know. We might be the only people in this whole area who haven't been captured by them. And now they're coming after us. I'm not interested in seeing if they want to be friends. We're gonna get this generator running, and then we're gonna get out of here, and you're going to help us."

"That is indeed the plan," Alexa said steadily. "I think your idea is much more exciting than waiting around back here, and I've never been part of a team before. From the story you told, you all sound quite resourceful."

Nina exchanged glances with Steve and Jack. This girl really did seem to be driven mostly by whatever seemed like the most intriguing option at any given time. It was as if she treated her life like a video game. Of course, if they could use that to their advantage, Nina probably shouldn't be too critical.

"There's only one problem," Alexa went on. "Whoever designed this backup generator system failed to take into account that to reach the generator, someone has to take the elevator, which runs on electricity."

Nina frowned. "So you're telling us . . ."

"We'll have to force open the door and climb down the shaft," Alexa stated matter-of-factly.

A loud, metallic clang echoed into the room from down the hallway through which they'd arrived, followed by one of the alien voices from before, so loud it was as if it were right there in the room with them.

"Oh no," Alexa sighed. "It was a clever plan, but I think we may be running out of time."

CHAPTER 12

"Screw the generator, we've got to get out of here!" Jack shouted.

Nina had to agree with Jack on this one. Frantically, she scanned the room around them. "Alexa, is there another way out?" Another deafening clang echoed down the hallway, this time accompanied by the sound of metal being ripped apart. "And don't tell me we have to make some kind of excavator out of this stuff and dig a tunnel—we have to go *now!*"

"No, not at all. There's a ventilation shaft behind one of the shelving units in here—I've been studying the blueprints to pass the time," Alexa explained coolly, clearly not picking up on the panic of the others. She tapped her finger against her mouth. "I don't remember which shelf though."

Steve jumped to his feet and scooped a flashlight off the table with his good arm. "Everybody grab a light! If we make it out of here we're gonna have to run, and I've already been knocked around enough stumbling through this mall in the dark."

"Alexa, you have to remember," Nina insisted. "Which shelf is the vent behind?"

Alexa began tapping her foot against the ground. "You know, it just didn't seem important at the time so I didn't bother to memorize exactly where it was. As you might recall, I was planning on meeting the Visitors, not running away from them."

There was another metallic groan from down the hallway as the door to systems and maintenance continued to give way to the Visitors' onslaught. Jack grabbed a flashlight off the table and clicked it on. "Well, you might not be used to this, Alexa, but I've taken enough multiple choice tests in my life to know that sometimes you just have to use the process of elimination," he shouted. He began tearing down one of the shelving units, sending tools and bottles of cleaner flying as it crashed onto the ground.

Steve and Nina quickly followed suit, each using their good arm to push the shelving units to the ground. An alien howl tore through the room, almost deafening them.

"There!" Nina shouted, pointing to a newly exposed metal grate embedded in the wall.

Jack ran up to it, threaded his fingers through the metal, and tore it clean out of the wall. He tossed the grate aside just as a smashing sound alerted them that the Visitors had managed to break through the doorway. "After this, I am definitely getting some snacks!" he shouted. "Now come on—let's get out of here!"

Nina clambered into the ventilation duct and Alexa followed along behind her. "Sorry buddy, this is gonna be a tight squeeze," Nina heard Jack say to Steve. A moment later she heard Jack throw himself into the ventilation shaft and Steve let out a small yelp. Jack must be dragging Steve along—hopefully by his good arm.

Nina's hand burned as the gash on her palm reopened. She kept crawling through the duct, leaving a slick trail of blood behind.

"Hurry!" Steve called from the rear. "I see something back there! Something really, really bad!"

Up ahead, Nina's flashlight beam caught another grated panel. She redoubled her efforts, pushing the pain out of her mind. She dragged herself onward until she reached the panel.

"Why are we stopping? Hey! Why are we stopping?" Steve shouted, panic taking over the edge of his voice.

"Hang on!" Nina shouted. She struggled to rearrange her body in the cramped crawlspace so that her feet were facing the grate. Then she began to kick. An alien voice echoed through the ventilation shaft behind them. *We don't have much time. They're hunting us.* Nina put all her strength into her next kick, and the grate gave way.

Nina dragged herself clear. Once again, she found herself in one of the mall's cavernous corridors. One part of the mall looked about the same as any others and it was difficult to say exactly where they were within the building, but anywhere was better than being stuck in Systems and Maintenance with the Visitors. She turned and reached down to help the others get free of the crawl space.

"Not good, not good, not good," Jack kept repeating as he struggled to free himself. With the help of Nina and Alexa, he was able to get out. Then he hauled Steve out into the open with one hand. They broke into a sprint, tearing down the corridor and dodging benches, massage tables, and hat kiosks as they went.

"Hey, Jack," Steve panted, "if we don't make it out of this . . . thanks. You're not that bad of a guy when it comes down to it."

"Not now, weirdo!" Jack snapped. "We can talk about this later, like actually any time other than right now."

Nina spotted a clothing shop up ahead filled with fake palm trees and other jungle decorations. "In here!" she whisper-shouted, breaking toward the entrance.

They staggered into the plastic jungle and quickly shut off their flashlights, panting in the darkness.

"What now?" Alexa asked quietly.

"I don't know," Nina admitted. She peered out from behind the leaves of a fake plastic tree so that she could get a view of the mall's main space. Off in the distance she could see beams of blue light cutting through the air, accompanied by voices screaming in an unfamiliar alien language.

CHAPTER 13

"Nina," Steve whispered suddenly, "if this goes the way I think it's gonna go, there's something I want to ask you."

"Steve, can you shut up!" Jack hissed. "You're going to get us killed."

It really was not the time, but Nina realized that, if things kept going the way they had been, it was never going to be. The Visitors hadn't had much trouble tracking them so far. Nina didn't have high hopes that the group could avoid capture much longer.

She turned to Steve. "What is it?"

The beams of light down the hallway continued to approach, although they were going excruciatingly slowly. Some kind of strange hissing squawks sounded through the halls as well. Steve glanced at the hall and then shakily turned back to Nina. "I just wanted to make sure we were okay," he said quietly. "Every time I try to make things better, I just screw them up, so if this is really the end, I wanted to . . ."

"Seriously?" Jack hissed again. "Not now, guys."

"Quiet," Alexa whispered. "This is obviously important, and we're much more likely to survive if everyone is emotionally stable."

An alien roar echoed through the shopping mall from somewhere nearby, and it was answered by another, farther off. There was another hissing squawk.

Nina gave a nervous laugh, running her good hand through her hair that was damp with sweat. "I mean, we're not okay. We're stuck in an abandoned shopping mall being chased by aliens. I can't think of a way for things to be less okay."

Steve gave her a worried look, and she smiled softly at him to calm him. "But you and me, we're fine. The dating thing didn't work out, but I'm always going to care about you."

He grunted. "Yeah, but that still kind of sucks. I'm sorry I messed everything up. And now it sucks even more because everything is so weird all the time."

"I know. But if, somehow, we both live for more than a few more minutes, it's going to suck a little less every day until it doesn't suck anymore. And it'll just be us, Nina and Steve, friends again, like old times."

The call and response of monstrous roars continued to grow nearer, as did the blue lights.

"You know, this has been lovely," Alexa whispered. "It probably hasn't meant much to you, but it's nice for me to be a part of something, even for such a brief time. I really wish we all would have gotten to know one another sooner."

Nina grinned at her, while Jack let out a frustrated moan and stood up. "All right, you know what? If we're not going to commit to this hiding thing, then I say we rush them. I didn't stick around and fight last time I had the chance, and I'm not going to make that mistake again." He released a long, shaky breath. "I shouldn't have left everyone. I should have at least tried to make sure more people could have gotten away. And it seems like a surprise attack is our only shot of getting out of here alive, especially with you three chattering away like the world isn't ending."

Nina stood up too. Jack had a harsh sort of bluntness to him, but he was right. They'd gotten this far together, and if it was all going to end right now, they may as well go down swinging. Together. She grabbed Steve by the hand and pulled him to his feet. "You ready, Steve?"

"Yeah," he said, giving her hand a squeeze and then letting it drop. "Let's do it."

Alexa leapt to her feet as well. "What a surprise! I love it—we're like the three musketeers! You know, despite the title, there are actually four of them."

"All right, fine, great, let's do this!" Jack shouted, clearly losing his patience with all of them. He turned toward the shop doors and raised a fist. "This one is for Earth, you alien freaks!"

They burst out the entrance to the store and charged toward the blue lights, which swung toward them immediately, bright enough to strike them all completely blind.

CHAPTER 14

Nina threw her arm up before her eyes and tried to blink her vision back into focus, groaning in pain. She could hear the others doing the same.

"Are we dead?" she heard Steve ask.

"Did the aliens get us?" Jack asked.

"Sir! We've located the survivors—all three of them, plus one more female," a woman's voice barked from behind the blinding wall of lights. "Prepare for extraction."

There was a beep followed by a static-riddled squawk, and a distorted voice replied, "Affirmative. Eastern Egress is all clear for Pilgrims. Plymouth Rock, out."

Somebody grabbed Nina roughly by the

shoulder and began guiding her down the hallway. "All right kids, we've gotta get out of here, now! They're on our tail. Let's go! Keep your heads down!" the woman shouted. She looked over her shoulder as she walked them forward. "Baker, Incanto, cover the rear!"

Nina stumbled forward with the guidance of the unknown arm as her vision gradually came into focus. Gunfire erupted from somewhere behind them, followed by a chorus of alien roars. A soldier's radio went off, and Nina quickly recognized the hissing squawk they'd been hearing: it was actually the static call of the soldiers' radios. She glanced over and saw some heavily armored soldiers ushering the others along beside her, then spotted rays of sunlight streaming in through a door up ahead.

They burst out into the parking lot on the other side of the mall, where there was a large armored vehicle waiting for them a few yards from the door. The soldiers quickly threw them in the back end of it before slamming the door shut and pounding on the rear window. The vehicle immediately sped off.

There was a medic in back, and she began checking their vitals. "Everyone okay?" she asked without looking up from her tools.

Nina found her voice first. "Yes," she said. "Yes, I think we're okay. What's going on? I mean, what even happened?"

"We don't know yet. They hit us hard and fast, but we got a lot of people out in time. Your families are looking for you—they noticed you were missing once we got back to the base," the medic explained. "Lucky for us we keep some hardware in a hardened bunker in case we get into a nuke fight—radios, lights, vehicles, everything. As soon as we can get more organized, we're gonna make the Visitors sorry they ever showed up."

Everyone was quiet for a few minutes as she checked each of their wounds. As she fitted Steve with an actual sling, the medic looked up at them and asked, "How'd you kids manage to make it on your own, anyway? It's a nightmare out here."

"Together," Nina said, smiling at the others. "We made it together."

ATTACK ON EARTH

WHEN ALIENS INVADE, ALL YOU CAN DO IS SURVIVE.

DESERTED

THE FALLOUT

THE FIELD TRIP

GETTING HOME

LOCKDOWN

TAKE SHELTER

CHECK OUT ALL THE TITLES IN THE
ATTACK ON EARTH SERIES

LEVEL UP

WHAT WOULD YOU DO IF YOU WOKE UP IN A VIDEO GAME?

ALIEN INVASION
ISRAEL KEATS

LABYRINTH
ISRAEL KEATS

POD RACER
R.T. MARTIN

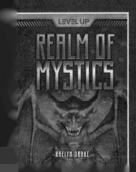

REALM OF MYSTICS
RAELYN DRAKE

SAFE ZONE
R.T. MARTIN

THE ZEPHYR CONSPIRACY
ISRAEL KEATS

DAY OF DISASTER

Would you survive?